BECKY HICKOX AYRES

MATRESHKA

Illustrated by Alexi Natchev

A Doubleday Book for Young Readers

A Doubleday Book for Young Readers
Published by
Delacorte Press
Bantam Doubleday Dell Publishing Group, Inc.
666 Fifth Avenue
New York, New York 10103

Library of Congress Cataloging-in-Publication Data
Ayres, Becky.
Matreshka / Becky Hickox Ayres; illustrated by Alexi Natchev.
p.   cm.
Summary: Kata's little wooden doll saves her life
when she is captured by Baba Yaga.
ISBN 0-385-30657-1
1. Baba Yaga (Legendary character)—Juvenile literature.
[1. Baba Yaga (Legendary character)   2. Fairy tales.
3. Folklore—Soviet Union.]   I. Natchev, Alexi, ill.   II. Title.
PZ8.A96Mat 1992
398.2—dc20   [E]   91-36359   CIP   AC

Manufactured in Hong Kong
October 1992

10 9 8 7 6 5 4 3 2 1

For my daughter, Rebecca Lynn

MANY YEARS AGO in the forests of Russia lived an old man with his granddaughter, Kata. Sometimes Kata walked the long path to the town of Vyatka to trade Grandfather's wooden spoons and bowls for food. One day in late autumn as she was returning from such a trip she saw a woman coming slowly down the path toward her. "Please," said the woman, "do you have any food to spare?"

When Kata gave her a loaf of bread and a piece of cheese, the woman handed her something in return. "Here," she said, "take this little wooden doll. I carved and painted her myself. Her name is Matreshka."

Kata tucked the doll into her apron and started out again. Darkness came early as storm clouds gathered.

Large snowflakes began sifting through the canopy of fir, and soon the ground was covered and the air thick. For several hours she struggled on as the wind grew wilder and colder, until at last she saw a faint light flickering through the trees. With the last of her strength, she forced her near-frozen feet to carry her closer.

It was a house—the strangest she had ever seen. It stood on giant chicken legs and was surrounded by a high wooden fence. She stumbled through the open gate and knocked at the door. A tall, thin woman opened it.

"Come in, child!" she exclaimed as she pulled Kata into the kitchen with her long, bony fingers. "It is a lucky thing that you happened upon Baba Yaga's house. I am the only one who lives in this part of the forest. Warm yourself by the stove and drink some tea while I build a fire in the guest room."

As soon as the woman left, Kata heard a muffled little voice. "Let me out!" it said. She looked about but saw no one.

"Let me out!" the voice insisted again.

Finally she realized that the voice came from her pocket. It was the wooden doll. Kata lifted Matreshka from her apron, and the doll hopped close to the fire, holding out her tiny hands to the warmth.

I was as cold as I could be.
Now may I please have a little tea?

Kata held the glass down to her, and the doll took dainty sips, but she jumped back into the apron pocket when Baba Yaga returned.

"There now, all ready. You must be very tired. Let me show you to your room."

The old woman led Kata up the stairs and down several long halls to a small room where she fell into an exhausted sleep.

When the bright sun woke her, Kata hurried to the door of her room to be on her way, but it wouldn't open.

"Help!" she called through the little window in the door.

Baba Yaga appeared a few moments later, but instead of opening the door she peered through the window and laughed.

"What? Wanting to leave so soon? I'm afraid you can't. The ingredients for my magic spell are not quite ready, but don't worry, my dear, it won't take long. I do believe you'll make a lovely goose for next Sunday's dinner."

After Baba Yaga's face disappeared from the window Kata pulled and tugged on the door, but it wouldn't budge.

"Let *me* try," said the little voice from her apron.

Kata lifted Matreshka from her pocket. "How can you open the door if I can't?"

The doll replied,
Matreshka, Matreshka,
I may be small,
But I'm just as handy
as someone tall.
Lift me up to see
out of the door,
And in a moment
we may know more.

Kata set the doll in the
window of the door.
Matreshka leaned out,
then hopped about in
excitement.

Ha! There is the latch
holding the key.
If I could reach it,
I'd set us free.

"Here," said Kata, "I'll tie
my scarf around you and
lower you down."

Within moments the door was open, and Kata stood in the hallway wondering which way to go. All the doors looked just alike, and the first one she opened screeched so loudly on its hinges that the dog in the yard started barking.

"If only you were a bit smaller," she said to Matreshka, "you would be able to roll under each door and find the way out."

The doll winked and said,

Matreshka, Matreshka,
I'm oh so small,
But not the smallest
one of all.

With that, Matreshka spun around three times, popped open for a moment, and out hopped another Matreshka doll, smaller than the first.

She scurried down the hall, rolling under each door until she found the one to the stairs. Kata opened it very slowly, and they tiptoed down to the kitchen.

The witch was not to be seen, and the door to the yard stood open. They crept to the fence, but here they found the gate locked tight with no key this time. Just then the dog barked again, and Baba Yaga came running from the forest behind the house with a basket of mushrooms.

"Oh, Matreshkas," cried Kata. "If only one of you were a little smaller, you could put your arm inside the keyhole and perhaps undo the lock."

With this, the second Matreshka said,

Matreshka, Matreshka, I'm oh so small,
But not the smallest one of all.

She spun around three times, and out popped a
third doll, smaller than the second. Kata lifted her
up to the keyhole, and the third Matreshka had it
open in a moment.

Kata scooped up the three dolls and ran into the woods, but the witch was soon close enough to cast a binding spell that made it impossible for Kata to run any farther. She watched helplessly as Baba Yaga laid a circle of magic rope all around her and the dolls.

"There now," cackled the witch, "no one inside the magic circle can step over the rope, and only someone on the outside can move it. So I guess you'll stay put while I go back to get the things I need to turn you into a goose."

Kata and the dolls tried for several minutes to step over the rope, but they could not.

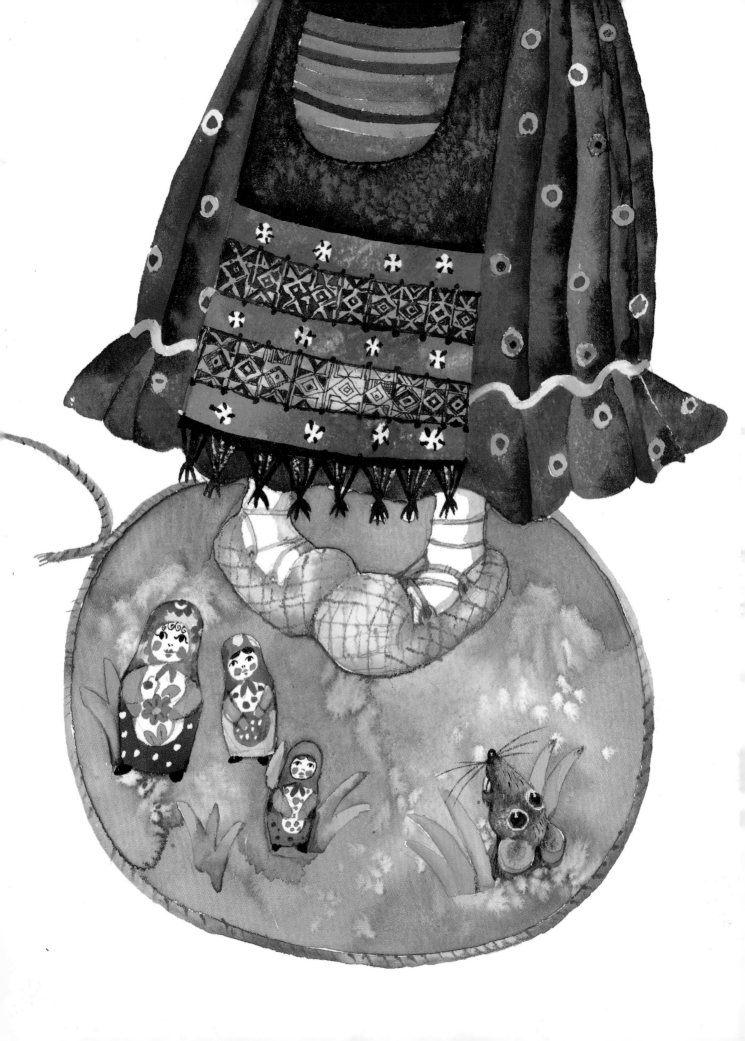

"Oh, Matreshkas," sighed Kata, "if only one of you were a little smaller, you could climb down this mouse hole and find a way to the other side."

The third Matreshka clapped her tiny hands and said,

Matreshka, Matreshka, I'm oh so small,
But not the smallest one of all.

She spun around, opened up, and out hopped an even smaller doll. This fourth Matreshka crawled into the hole. Although she went as fast as she could, they could hear Baba Yaga returning by the time the doll had appeared at the other end of the burrow just beyond the magic circle. She quickly opened the circle of rope, but before Kata could go three steps, Baba Yaga's magic once again brought her to a stop. Now the witch was in a rage.

"You miserable child! I'll not wait for Sunday. I'll have you for dinner tonight!"

Just as Baba Yaga started chanting her magic spell, Kata saw the fourth Matreshka moving her lips and spinning.

Matreshka, Matreshka, I'm oh so small,
But we need the smallest one of all.

The last Matreshka was no taller than a thumbnail. She scrambled up Baba Yaga's dress, perched in her ear, and began whispering. This confused the witch, and she kept muddling the words of her spell.

Chinkita, pinkita, magic juice,
I now turn Taka into a goose.

But of course since Baba Yaga had said the name wrong, Kata did not turn into a goose.

Baba Yaga's temper increased. She stamped her
foot and tried again.

Hennery, pennery, whirl and twirl,
I now turn Kata into a girl.

This didn't work either. By now Baba Yaga was red all over, and she screamed the next spell with the smallest Matreshka still whispering in her ear.

Floppity, moppity, grin and grog,
Baba Yaga is now a frog.

This time the spell did work. As all the Matreshkas hopped back together and into Kata's pocket, a very angry frog bounded away.

Later that day Kata found the path leading back to her grandfather's cottage. From that time on she spent many happy hours playing with the little wooden dolls, and although Kata never again got lost in the forest, she always carried Matreshka in her pocket just in case.

ABOUT THE AUTHOR

Becky Hickox Ayres is a high school librarian who has written two books for children, *Victoria Flies High,* a picture book illustrated by Robin Koontz, and *Salt Lake City,* a work of nonfiction. She lives with her husband and daughter in Keizer, Oregon.

ABOUT THE ILLUSTRATOR

Alexi Natchev has illustrated many books for children and adults in his native Bulgaria. He is also a printmaker and has been a professor of drawing at the Academy of Arts in Sofia. He is now living in Moscow, Idaho, with his wife and son.

ABOUT THE BOOK

The illustrations for this book were painted with Windsor Newton watercolors and various mixed media on Strathmore Imperial paper.

The book is set in 24-point ITC Usherwood Book. The typography is by Lynn Braswell.